My dear mouse friends,

Have I ever told you how much I love science fiction? I've always wanted to write incredible adventures set in another dimension, but I've never believed that parallel universes exist . . . until now!

That's because my good friend Professor Paws von Volt, the brilliant, secretive scientist, has just made an incredible discovery. Thanks to some mousetropic calculations, he determined that there are many different dimensions in time and space, where anything could be possible.

The professor's work inspired me to write this science fiction adventure in which my family and I travel through space in search of new worlds. We're a fabumouse crew: the spacemice!

I hope you enjoy this intergalactic adventure!

Geronimo Stilton

**PROFESSOR
PAWS VON VOLT**

THE SPACEMICE

GERONIMO STILTONIX

TRAP STILTONIX

THEA STILTONIX

GRANDFATHER WILLIAM STILTONIX

ROBOTIX

BENJAMIN STILTONIX AND BUGSY WUGSY

Geronimo Stilton

WE'LL BITE YOUR TAIL, GERONIMO!

Scholastic Inc.

Published by Scholastic Inc., *Publishers since 1920*, 557 Broadway, New York, NY 10012. SCHOLASTIC and associated logos are trademarks and/or registered trademarks of Scholastic Inc.

ISBN 978-1-338-15919-6

Text by Geronimo Stilton
Original title *E poi ti mordicchio la coda, Stiltonix!*
Cover by Flavio Ferron
Illustrations by Giuseppe Facciotto (pencils), Carolina Livio (inks), and Valeria Cairoli and Paolo Vicenzi (color)
Graphics by Marta Lorini

Special thanks to AnnMarie Anderson
Translated by Lidia Morson Tramontozzi
Interior design by Kevin Callahan/BNGO Books

10 9 8 7 6 5 4 3 2 1   17 18 19 20 21

Printed in the U.S.A.   40
First printing 2017

In the darkness of the farthest galaxy in time and space is a spaceship inhabited exclusively by mice.

This fabumouse vessel is called the **MouseStar 1**, and I am its captain!

I am Geronimo Stiltonix, a somewhat accident-prone mouse who (to tell you the truth) would rather be writing novels than steering a spaceship.

But for now, my adventurous family and I are busy traveling around the universe on exciting intergalactic missions.

THIS IS THE LATEST ADVENTURE OF THE SPACEMICE!

A Quiet Afternoon . . . Or Was It?

It all started on a quiet Sunday afternoon. I had promised my nephew Benjamin I would take him to the premier of The Fleeing Spaceships, the last movie in the Lord of the Asteroids trilogy. This episode would finally end the epic **search** for the lost asteroid!

Oops! I'm so sorry . . . I forgot to introduce myself. My name is Stiltonix, Geronimo Stiltonix. I am the captain of the legendary *MouseStar 1,* the most mousestastic spaceship in the whole universe, though honestly, my real dream is to become a **writer**. But that's another story!

5-D MEGA MOUSERIFIC MOVIE

This five-dimensional movie takes place in a special circular screening room. Moviegoers strap themselves into special extra-comfy moving seats. Then holograms seem to emerge from the screen and float around the room while the superstellar surround-sound system kicks into high gear. **Warning:** 5-D mega mouserific movies are not recommended for anyone who is a jittery scaredy-mouse!

Now, what was I squeaking about? Oh, right! My nephew and I were so excited to see the new 5-D Lord of the Asteroids movie, we got to the theater early.

"Look, Uncle G!" Benjamin exclaimed. "There's Trap, **Bugsy Wugsy**, Thea, Grandfather William, and SALLY. Let's sit with them!"

Mousey meteorites! Sally de Wrench was the most fabumouse rodent in the **CHEDDAR GALAXY**, and there was an empty seat right next to her! I quickly headed for that seat, but as I got closer, my paws became **mushier than melted cheese**, my mouth dried up, and I heard a strange buzzing in my ears. I was galactically nervous! Luckily, by the time I got to the seat, the lights had dimmed and the first **hologram** had come shooting out of the screen. I was about to relax when . . .

AAAAAAAHHH!!!

We heard a fur-raising scream that made the room tremble.

"W-what was that?" I stammered.

"It sounded like it came from Professor Greenfur's cabin next door!" Sally exclaimed.

We rushed out of the movie and went to check on the professor. When he opened his door, we were **stunned**.

"Professor Greenfur, w-what happened?" I asked.

"I don't know," he replied **SaDLy**. "When I looked in the mirror, this is what I saw!"

"You're orange!" squeaked Benjamin.

Shooting stars! In case you don't know, true to his name, the professor's fur is usually **green**! But now he was more **ORANGE** than an apricot from Uranus.

"Did you eat an **ALIEN DISH**

What's happening to me?

at the Space Yum Café?" Trap asked. "Sometimes Cook Squizzy puts in too many space spices . . ."

"Are you working too hard?" bellowed Grandfather William. "Lack of sleep can make you sick!"

"Maybe you used a new soap or cream?" Thea suggested. "One time, my fur got the craziest pink spots . . ."

Professor Greenfur shook his head.

"Nope," he replied, dejected. "I haven't done anything out of the ordinary."

Holey craters! We had to figure out what was causing his STRANGE condition!

I Have the Answer!

Benjamin and Bugsy Wugsy scurried to the **control room**. They used the ship's onboard computer, Hologramix, to search for any available information on the planet **PHOTOSYNTHESON**, which is where Professor Greenfur was born.

The rest of us stayed with the scientist, hoping to distract him a bit.

"How are you *feeling*?" asked Trap. "Are you *hungry*?"

"Actually, yes," the professor replied. "Now that you mention it, I'm cosmically hungry. I could really go for some *SOUP*!"

"Excellent choice!" Trap replied. "I'll call Squizzy on my wristwatch phone and I'll ask him to prepare some whisker-licking good

MARTIAN GINGER soup for you. You'll love it!"

Then we hopped in an astrotaxi and headed to the SPACE YUM CAFÉ. When we got there, Cook Squizzy came out to meet us. He was carrying a gigantic pot of orange soup.

"Martian ginger soup is the best remedy for itching caused by Venus allergies, nausea from hyperspace jumping, and space fevers!" he squeaked.

Then he filled a huge bowl and motioned to Professor Greenfur to drink it up. We stared open-mouthed as the scientist drank the entire **bowl** in one gulp.

"Ahhhh!" Professor Greenfur sighed. "That was truly mouserific. Thank you!"

But unfortunately, nothing happened. The professor was still orange!

"I should have put in more **molded space cheese**," Cook Squizzy said sadly.

"Of course not, **SQUIZZY**," Thea said, smiling. "Even if your soup didn't cure him, I'm sure it made Professor Greenfur feel a little **better**. Right?"

"I'm not sure," he answered slowly. "Maybe I should move around a little to

Slurp!

help my digestion. I'm feeling bloated."

"Don't worry," my sister said. "I have the answer!"

Then she had dragged us all to the multipurpose technogym.

"You can do all the moving around you want right here!" she squeaked happily.

"Grandson, you should **JOIN** him!" my grandfather suggested immediately. "You should really be exercising more often. I want you to be in tip-top shape, just like a real captain!"

"I *am* a real captain," I protested. "And I exercise plenty. Plus, I feel **great**!"

But putting up a fight was useless.

An astrosecond later, I found myself running alongside Professor Greenfur on the galactic treadmill. After that, we did **abdominal crunches**. Finally,

Grandfather William had us each do one hundred *push-ups*.

Galactic Gorgonzola! It was HARD WORK! After all that exercising, Professor Greenfur was still as ORANGE as ever!

"How do you feel now?" my sister asked hopefully. "Any different?"

"Yes," he replied, gasping for air. "I feel sore ALL OVER! What I need now is a MASSAGE!"

"I have the perfect solution," Sally explained. "The massagemousix.

It's a device that gives the most mousetastic massages in the **solar system**! After spending a day fixing motors, a massagemousix treatment always makes me feel ***AMAZING***."

"Excellent!" squeaked an exhausted-looking Professor Greenfur.

Sally led the professor into a small room just off the technogym and had him lie down on a high-tech table.

When the Professor activated the massagemousix, **four long mechanical arms** popped out and began to vigorously MASSAGE his sore body.

There was an empty spot right next to the professor. I was about to ask Sally if I could try the massagemousix myself when my cousin dove for the table.

"I could really use a good massage!" he

SQUEAKED. "Geronimo, watching you and the professor work out was **exhausting**! In fact, I could really go for an ENERGIZING four-cheese shake from Uranus. Geronimo, could you grab one for me from the Space Yum Café?"

Shooting stars! My cousin was TOO MUCH!

Er . . .
How relaxing!

I was about to tell him I absolutely would not fetch him a cheese shake when I heard my nephew Benjamin's sweet voice.

"Uncle G!" he squeaked excitedly. "Bugsy and I found a ton of **USEFUL INFORMATION**! And we know why Professor Greenfur turned orange!"

DON'T JUST
STAND THERE!

"Bugsy Wugsy and I did some research in the **Encyclopedia Galactica**," Benjamin explained.

"We discovered that **plant mouseoids** from Photosyntheson turn orange when

From the Encyclopedia Galactica
PHOTOSYNTHESONS

Photosynthesons are plant mouseoids born on the planet Photosyntheson. These green creatures have a special bond with their home planet for their entire life. No matter how far away they are, if danger threatens their native land, they turn orange.

something's wrong on their home planet," Bugsy Wugsy added.

"A problem on PHOTOSYNTHESON?" Professor Greenfur whispered, alarmed. "I left the planet with my parents when I was very little, but I have to go back to help!"

"Professor, how FAR is Photosyntheson from here?" asked Thea.

"According to my calculations, it's about THREE GALACTIC HOURS away," he replied.

"Well, what are you waiting for, Grandson?" Grandfather William bellowed. "Don't just stand there—take action! Alert the crew that you're going on an important mission to Photosyntheson RIGHT AWAY!"

Solar smoked Gouda! Why did my grandfather have to be so BOSSY? Of course I would organize a mission immediately.

After all, I was the ship's **captain**! I cleared my throat.

"Er, attention, spacemice!" I squeaked. "We will leave as soon as possible on a mission to **photosyntheson**. Once we arrive, a crew of spacemice will explore the planet to find out what's going on. **PROFESSOR GREENFUR** will be **GREEN** again in no time!"

Everyone cheered.

"Can we come, too?" Benjamin and Bugsy Wugsy squeaked in unison.

"That's the spirit!" Grandfather William **smiled**. "You should learn from these eager young mouselets, Geronimo. They didn't waste a moment before they volunteered!"

I sighed and tried to ignore my grandfather.

"Of course you can come," I told Benjamin

and Bugsy. "Next stop, **Photosyntheson!**"

Professor Greenfur, Benjamin, Bugsy Wugsy, Thea, Sally, Trap, and I began to prepare for the mission. But wait . . . where **WAS** Trap?! I looked around and realized my cousin had disappeared. Could he have gone to the Space Yum Café to get his ENERGiZiNG CHEESE SHaKE? Suddenly, my cousin reappeared. But instead of carrying a cheese shake, he was dragging an enormouse backpack with a **ZiLLiON** pockets.

Mousey meteorites! It looked heavy!

"Trap, where did you go?" I asked. "We're getting ready for our mission to Photosyntheson—"

"I figured," he interrupted me. "That's why I went to get a few **indispensable** little things you'll need on your mission!"

A few little things? My mission?!

"What do you mean? You're coming with me!"

"No, I'm not." He chuckled. "I'm staying right here."

"WHAT?!"

"You heard me," he explained. "I'm staying put! You're not the only **WRITER** aboard *MouseStar 1*, Cuz. I'm writing a book, too!"

"**A BOOK?!?**" I squeaked, incredulous. Trap wasn't exactly a regular in the *MouseStar 1*'s library.

"Yes!" Trap exclaimed proudly. "It's called *A Mousestastic Guide to Galactic Restaurants*. It's a guide for space foodies, and I'm on a deadline, so I can't come. But relax! I packed everything you'll need. You'll be fine!"

With that, he tossed me the backpack. I staggered under its enormouse weight.

"*SQUEEEAK!*" I yelped. "It's really **heavy**!"

"Don't be such a wimp, Grandson!" Grandfather William scolded me. "A **real captain** doesn't complain!"

Squeeeak!

"It's time to go," Thea interrupted us. "The **space shuttle** is ready for departure. The planet Photosyntheson awaits!"

AT THE SPEED OF LIGHT!

"I'm programming the ship to travel at the *speed of light*," Thea announced once we were all aboard. "So hold on to your tails! Destination: Photosyntheson!"

HOLEY CRATERS! I'll never get used to traveling at the speed of light. Just hearing those words made my tail knot up like a **space cheese pretzel**!

Speed of light!

I clung tightly to my seat and tried to take a deep breath.

MOUSEY METEORITES! I felt incredibly nauseous! I was afraid I might toss my cheese!

After what felt like a light-year, Thea turned things down a notch.

"I'm disengaging the speed of light and will proceed at supersonic speed," she explained.

I sighed in relief. I could finally relax and enjoy the view.

Stars and multicolored planets shone all around us. Cosmic space dust, what a fabumouse view!

"There's Photosyntheson!" squeaked Benjamin.

The planet ahead of us was truly beautiful. It was a brilliant green and, from afar, it looked like a gigantic HEAD OF LETTUCE!

We all crowded around the window to see better.

"Look!" exclaimed Bugsy Wugsy. "The surface is completely covered with **trees**."

"Wow!" Benjamin squeaked. "There are so many different kinds!"

"I'm finally going to see my home again," Professor Greenfur whispered. There were happy tears in his eyes.

Thea smiled.

"Everyone back to your seats," she ordered. "We're about to **LAND**!"

WELCOME TO PHOTOSYNTHESON!

Thea gently landed the space shuttle in a soft green meadow in Photosyntheson's **astroport**.

"We're here!" squeaked my sister. "Welcome home, Professor!"

Benjamin and Bugsy Wugsy were the first to disembark.

"What an awesome planet!" my nephew exclaimed. "It feels like we're in an enormouse NATURAL RESERVE!"

Professor Greenfur looked around, squeakless. He was so overwhelmed at returning to the planet where he had been born. He **BREATHED** in deeply, filling his lungs joyfully.

I smiled at him. It was truly **MOVING** to see him so happy at his return to his home planet.

A moment later, Bugsy Wugsy broke the silence. "Look!" she shouted. "Someone's coming!"

We saw a group of **PHOTOSYNTHESONS** approaching. Some looked almost identical to Professor Greenfur, while others were much shorter or had colorful flowers

Welcome!

on their heads. But all had brilliant green fur!

"Welcome, Spacemice!" a DISTINCTIVE-LOOKiNG Photosyntheson greeted us kindly.

"Your ship's computer let us know you were coming," he said. "I'm Leafyfur, the governor of Photosyntheson. It's an honor for us to have a visit from the famous space captain Geronimo Stiltonix!"

Me? A famous captain? Huh?! A little old plant mouseoid with *tiny violets* sprouting out of her head came closer to the professor.

"Gentiana, look!" she exclaimed. "It's Greenfur!"

The Photosyntheson near her squeaked. "Cosmic roots!" she gasped. "You're right, Violix!"

Gentiana turned back to Greenfur. "My, how you've changed!" she said.

Greenfur! How you've grown!

"Er . . . I . . ." stammered Greenfur.

"We're your old tree neighbors, **Violix** and **GENTIANA**!" she continued. "I remember when you

Violix   Gentiana

used to sleep in a tiny little **VASE**. And now look at you! You've grown so **tall**."

"Forgive me for asking," Violix said softly. "But why are you so ⊙ra̋ṅg̈e?"

"Unfortunately, he turned orange because there's a problem on Photosyntheson," Thea explained. "When plant mouseoids leave your planet, they become orange if something **THREATENS** their home planet. Have you noticed anything

out of the ordinary lately?"

Leafyfur shook his head, surprised.

"No," he said. "Everything here has been very PEACEFUL! Come, see for yourself!"

Leafyfur, Violix, and Gentiana led us on a quick tour of the planet. It was INCREDIMOUSE. It seemed as though peace and harmony reigned everywhere. Could Benjamin and Bugsy Wugsy have misread the *Encyclopedia Galactica*?

It began growing dark. Leafyfur invited us to spend the night at his house. So we said good-night to Violix and Gentiana.

"I'm honored to have you as my guests," the governor squeaked. "My palace is bright, spacious, and surrounded by LUSH, GREEN plants!"

Leafyfur's Palace

I loved the idea of spending a night in a PALACE. I had carried the ENORMOUSE BACKPACK Trap had given me for the entire day. I felt like a **limp** slice of Swiss. I was already drooling at the prospect of a delicious DINNER followed by a long sleep in a SOFt, comfortable bed. But as soon as we arrived, I got a shock: Leafyfur's palace was indeed surrounded by nature. It was in a very TALL tree!

MOUSEY METEORS! To get to the palace, we had to climb all the way to the top! Leafyfur led the way.

"Follow me," he squeaked as he scampered up easily. "Welcome to my home!"

Thea, Greenfur, Benjamin, and Bugsy

Wugsy scooted up the tree. But I hung back, **TERRIFIED**. I'm so scared of heights!

"Come on, Geronimo!" my sister shouted.

Looking **UP** at the tall tree turned my stomach upside down and inside out. Besides, I was still wearing Trap's **heavy backpack**, which was going to make the climb even harder!

How did I always get myself into these situations?

Trying to be brave, I took the first step. But the heavy backpack made me tip backward, and I fell on my **tail**.

"Oooouch!" I cried.

Luckily, Leafyfur **threw** me a rope.

"Grab the rope, Captain," he called down. "We'll pull you up in no time! **Hold on tight!**"

I grabbed the rope and took a deep breath. But before I could **exhale**, the elastic rope

Hold on tight!

retracted and I flew **upward** at the speed of light. Galactic Gorgonzola! What a fright!

I landed on my back right in front of the door. My friends stifled their *GIGGLES* as they helped me up. I was

greener than moldy Brie, but at least I hadn't tossed my cheese!

Leafyfur welcomed us inside.

"Please sit down," he said warmly. "Dinner will be served shortly. We'll have Photosyntheson's **specialties**: moss bruschetta, root soup, and WILD BERRY pie."

Aaaaaaah!

"Yum!" Greenfur said happily. "My favorite comfort foods!"

But I was still **NAUSEOUS** from my trip up to the top of the tree. I had no desire to eat **ROOT SOUP**! On the other hand, I didn't want to be **rude**. So I tried to smile as I took a sip of the broth. **Blech!** It was **awful**.

Gulp!

MYSTERY AT EVERGREEN GROVE

The following morning, Leafyfur, Violix, and Gentiana took us to visit **Evergreen Grove**, where Greenfur had been born.

"Evergreen Grove is no longer ***inhabited*** today," Gentiana explained.

"Older residents like us moved to other parts of the planet, and the area became a **NATURAL** reserve," Violix added.

When we got there, we were squeakless.

Holey craters! It was fabumouse!

"Our best gardeners planted rare plants and trees all around the park," Violix continued. "Photosynthesons love coming here to walk, play, and relax in the shade of the trees."

Gentiana took us to the old tree in the center of the park, where Greenfur's family used to live. It was a big, tall tree with thick foliage. Greenfur smiled, tears filling his eyes.

"Sprouting tree seedlings!" he exclaimed. "It's just as I REMEMBERED it!"

We stood there quietly admiring

I remember it!

Huff, puff!

Awesome!

the **incredible** tree. I took that opportunity to slip off the **heavy backpack**. I wondered what

These trees are very rare!

This is where Greenfur was born!

was in that thing—it weighed a **TON**!

My back was so **sore** that I went to lean against the trunk of the tree for a little rest. I was so **exhausted**! But I had barely even touched the trunk when the entire tree fell to the ground with an enormouse **CRASH**!

The Photosynthesons looked at me in **horror**.

"Captain, what have you done?" Professor Greenfur asked.

"Um . . . I just leaned **g-gently** against the t-trunk," I stammered. "See?"

And I gently placed my paw on another trunk to demonstrate. But that tree *fell*, too! As it fell, it hit another tree, and then another. In just a few **astroseconds**, the entire grove of trees had fallen like a bunch of **DOMINOES**.

MOUSEY METEORITES! What was going on?!

Um . . .

WHO DID THIS?

I couldn't escape the **GLARING EYES** of the Photosynthesons. They were all shooting daggers at me!

Leafyfur looked at me gravely.

"Captain Stiltonix, we welcomed you in friendship," he said. "But this disaster is testing our patience. Can you explain yourself?"

I didn't know what to say. I had barely touched those trees! And I'm not a very **STRONG** mouse. In fact, I'm really, really *weak*! That's why I had taken off that HEAVY BACKPACK and leaned against the tree. I just wanted a little rest!

I was so embarrassed. Why, oh why had my cousin given me such a **heavy backpack** to carry?!

"Uh . . . um . . ." I muttered, trying to figure out a way to **explain** myself.

Fortunately, Thea came to my rescue.

"Listen, my brother may be a *klutz*," she explained to Leafyfur, "but he would never do something like this on purpose!"

"Thea's right!" Greenfur cried suddenly. "Look what I just found!"

We all rushed to see what Professor Greenfur has discovered. By all the rings

of Saturn, the tree trunk was completely hollow!

"It looks like something **gnawed** the inside of all the trees!" Bugsy Wugsy squeaked.

"There's something strange going on here," Thea added. "I'm sure this is the reason Greenfur turned orange!"

Who did this?

It's a mystery!

"This is **terrible**," Leafyfur said sadly. "And we didn't notice anything!"

"These **TREES** are extremely important to us," Violix explained. "They clean the **air** we breathe, they provide us with food, and they are our **homes**. No Photosyntheson would ever do anything to hurt the trees in *Evergreen Grove*. Who could have done such a thing?"

"Don't worry," Thea said gently. "We'll help you solve this *mystery*. After all, that's why we came!"

"That's right!" I agreed, bravely trying to act like a captain. "Spacemice for one, spacemice for all!"

THE SEARCH BEGINS

Leafyfur and the other Photosynthesons went back to their homes while we gathered to organize our investigation.

"We should split up," Thea said. "Each of us can follow a different clue."

"Good idea!" Benjamin agreed. "Bugsy Wugsy and I will interview the PHOTOSYNTHESONS strolling in the park. Maybe one of them saw something suspicious!"

"Sounds good," Thea replied with a nod. "I'll go back to the space shuttle. I can use Hologramix to gather info on any galactic parasites that have passed through Photosyntheson."

"I'll use the sniffix to search for clues,"

Greenfur said. He took a small robot out of his pocket. It was equipped with a special **ODOR-SMELLING** duct. Greenfur set the robot in research mode and the sniffix immediately took off.

"What about you, Ger?" Thea asked me.

"I think I'll go with Professor Greenfur," I replied.

The sniffix moved around **RAPIDLY**,

From the Encyclopedia Galactica
THE SNIFFIX

This small robot has an **ULTRA-DEVELOPED** sense of smell and can collect the smallest traces of odors. The robot is equipped with tiny wheels that use cosmic propulsion to move over any terrain. It has an interactive screen and is capable of **talking to the spacemice**. Its one defect is that it's allergic to space pollen! It makes the robot **sneeze** and keeps it from working properly.

looking for clues. Charts, images, and calculations appeared continuously on its little screen. We scampered along behind the robot. I was wearing Trap's **heavy backpack** again and I was having a hard time keeping up!

Suddenly, the little robot stopped. But instead of showing us the results of his investigation, he began to sneeze.

"Holey craters!" I exclaimed. "What's going on?"

"ACHOO!" answered the sniffix in its metallic voice. "There are traces of SPACE POLLEN in the air. I'm allergic! I am sorry. I cannot elaborate on the data I have collected." Greenfur sighed.

"We have to get back to the space shuttle," he explained. "There must be some ROBOTIC ALLERGY MEDICINE on board the ship."

My shoulders were sore and ACHING from carrying Trap's backpack, so I decided to wait and take a rest while Professor Greenfur got the medicine. I removed the hEaVy backpack from my shoulders and sprawled out on the grass. Then I turned to my side and noticed a thin trail of sawdust winding through the blades of grass.

Martian mozzarella! Maybe I had found a clue!

THE MYSTERIOUS GNAWERS

I quickly scrambled to my paws and began to follow the **T R A I L**. It seemed to stop from time to time, but it always started up again. The trail went **straight**, then it curved, then it ZIG-ZAGGED across the grass.

How strange!

Hmmm . . . **What a strange trail!**

I was following the trail so **CLOSELY** I didn't realize I had left Evergreen Grove. I suddenly found myself in a part of Photosyntheson I didn't recognize. The trail ended in a CLEARING surrounded by tall bushes. I hid behind one and looked around. At first, I didn't see anything. Then I looked down and I was flabbergasted! The clearing was filled with **tiny** aliens scurrying in and out of small **HOLES** in the ground.

I studied them for a few more minutes. They had huge teeth and were busily chewing on something that left behind a trail of **sawdust**.

Solar smoked Gouda! These were the creatures who had gnawed all the trees in Evergreen Grove! **But why?**

I tried to observe a little more without being seen, but I inadvertently placed a paw on a twig. **Crack!**

As soon as they heard the noise, the little creatures stopped and looked around **suspiciously**. But I was well hidden behind the bush. Luckily, they didn't see me. After an **astrosecond** of hesitation, they went back to their chewing. *PHEW!* I was safe!

I watched the little aliens for a few more minutes. They were so **CUTE**, I decided I would just approach them and ask what they were doing. It couldn't hurt to be *friendly* and introduce myself, could it? So

I gathered my **COURAGE** and stepped out from behind the bush. I moved slowly so I wouldn't **startle** the creatures.

"Good morning, friends!" I squeaked in a friendly tone. "My name is Stiltonix, **Geronimo Stiltonix**, and I'm the captain of—"

I didn't even have a chance to **finish**. The little aliens surrounded me quickly. They had *menacing* looks on their unusual snouts.

"**Who** are you?" one of them asked.

"**What** do you want?" another growled.

Gnaw!

"And **why** are you here?" asked another.

Maybe introducing myself hadn't

been such a good idea after all!

"Er . . . as I was saying, I'm the captain of —"

But I didn't get to finish that time, either! Faster than a shooting star, the ALIENS tied me up.

MOUSEY METEORS! I WAS THEIR PRISONER!

THE NIBBLIX ALIENS

I shouted as loudly as I could, hoping the other Spacemice would hear me.

"Heeeelp!"

"Silence!" a voice commanded.

I didn't have to be told twice! A well-dressed alien with a wooden crown on his head poked me in the tummy. Martian mozzarella! He looked like their king. And he was **mad**!

The alien cleared his throat.

"I am Chief Nibbler the Fourth," he snorted. "I am Lord of the Underground and king of the nibblix aliens, who live in Photosyntheson's **subterranean** zone! Introduce yourself, you mouse in a spacesuit!"

Who are you?

"Er . . . as I tried telling you before, I'm Geronimo Stiltonix, **captain** of the *MouseStar 1*," I explained.

"Geronimo Stiltonix?!" he replied, surprised. "What are you doing on **Photosyntheson**?"

I cleared my throat.

"Nibbler, I came here with my friends the spacemice to figure out what's been happening on Photosyntheson," I explained. "Basically, we wanted to know who's been **gnawing** all the trees!"

"My name is Chief Nibbler the Fourth!" he roared back. "Or, 'YOUR MAJESTY'! No one dares to call me 'Nibbler'! That is, no one except my lovely wife . . ."

"I'm so sorry, Your Majesty!" I replied, trying to make up for my mistake. "Would you please tell me why you and your friends are gnawing all of Photosyntheson's trees?"

"We have our reasons!" bellowed Chief Nibbler. "We nibblix have always lived underneath Photosyntheson. Our big teeth help us dig tunnels and build underground villages where we used to live happily."

Everyone nodded in agreement.

"Unfortunately, one day we dug in the

wrong place, and there was a terrible **flood**," the chief continued. "Most of our homes were destroyed."

The nibblix aliens all nodded sadly.

"Fortunately, we were able to flee to the upper tunnels," Chief Nibbler continued. "But the lower tunnels are still flooded, and we're afraid the water level will keep **RiSiNG**! That's why we decided to move above ground."

Holey craters! What an incredible story!

Everything was beginning to make sense now. But there still was one thing I didn't understand.

"That's awful," I squeaked sympathetically. "But why are you nibblix gnawing on the trees?"

"Isn't it obvious?!" Chief Nibbler replied

gruffly. "Do you think these perfect sets of teeth stay like this on their own? We have to keep exercising our incisors to keep them from getting too **long** or too weak! When we're underground, we can keep busy gnawing the dirt. But above ground, there's nothing to chew on but trees!"

Look at this set of teeth!

I finally understood. The nibblix didn't mean to hurt the trees, but they didn't seem to have a **choice**!

"If it's true that you came to solve the **MYSTERY** of the trees, the solution is simple: **It was us!**" Chief Nibbler continued. "But we don't know what else to do. We have to keep our teeth **HEALTHY**, and we have no place to stay underground right now!"

GERONIMO, WHERE ARE YOU?

Meanwhile, Thea, Benjamin, Bugsy Wugsy, and Professor Greenfur were all back where we had parted. No one had found any useful information, and they returned to find me **MISSING**! My sister knew something was wrong right away.

"**LOOK!**" she squeaked. "This is the backpack Trap gave Geronimo! But where's my brother?"

"When I came to the ship in search of the **allergy medicine**, the captain told me he wanted to **rest**," Greenfur explained. "He must have started looking for clues. But it's strange that he left the backpack behind."

At that moment, Benjamin noticed the **trail of sawdust**.

"I wonder if Uncle Ger followed this trail," he said. "Let's see where it **LEADS!**"

Greenfur put on the backpack and they all followed the trail. When they came to the clearing, they hid in the bushes and peeked out at me and the nibblix aliens. They were horrified by what they saw.

Oh no!

"**oh no!**" squeaked Benjamin softly. "**They captured Uncle G!**"

"Don't worry!" Greenfur whispered reassuringly. "I'm sure we'll figure out a way to free him. Does anyone know what kind of aliens those are?"

Bugsy Wugsy didn't waste time. She contacted **HOLOGRAMIX** right away

From the Encyclopedia Galactica

NIBBLIX ALIENS

Where they're from:
Photosyntheson's subterranean zone

**Features: They
are short with
large, strong
teeth that need to
be used constantly!
That's why they
continuously dig long
tunnels underground.**

**Fun Facts: They have a sweet tooth!
When they're in a good mood, they love
to play pranks.**

Favorite Food: Sweets of every kind!

**Motto: *Look at our teeth, so healthy and strong;
We must keep gnawing all day long!***

using her wristwatch communicator.

She explained the situation, and an astrosecond later Hologramix sent her the data from the *Encyclopedia Galactica*.

Thea, Benjamin, and Professor Greenfur gathered around Bugsy Wugsy and read the info.

"Excellent work, Bugsy!" Thea exclaimed, patting the mouselet on the back. "This background info on the nibblix aliens gives me an idea as to how we can free Geronimo . . ."

A Familiar Aroma

I was so *busy* talking to the nibblix aliens about their PLIGHT that I didn't see the other spacemice in the bushes nearby.

Suddenly, the air filled with a **superstellar aroma**.

Galactic Gorgonzola!

Gnaw

Don't goooo!

I would have recognized that smell anywhere. It was the scent of a mouth-watering cheesecake! The nibblix began to sniff the air eagerly.

"Spacious subterranean tunnels!" the chief exclaimed. "What a smell! I'm famished. Nibblix, how about a SNACK? Let's follow that scent!"

The other aliens happily scurried after their leader.

Shooting stars! They were going without me!

"Wait! Don't goooo!" I shouted. "Don't leave me tied up here all **alooooone**!"

But the nibblix didn't listen. They were too busy following that **mousetastic** scent. In fact, I realized it wasn't the scent of just any old cheesecake. Instead, it was the smell of a very **SPECIaL** cheesecake: Chef Squizzy's famous **triple cheesecake** with **candied fruit** on top! Holey craters!

As soon as the nibblix were out of sight, I heard **movement** coming from the bushes behind me.

"**W-w-who's there?**" I stammered.

"It's us, Uncle G!" came my nephew's **SWEET** squeak.

Thank goodmouse! The Spacemice had come to my rescue!

A DELICIOUS IDEA

Thea, Greenfur, Benjamin, and Bugsy Wugsy came out of the bushes. They immediately began working to **untie** the ropes wrapped TIGHTLY around me.

"Prickly shrubs!" exclaimed Professor Greenfur. "What strong knots! Too bad I don't have my portable knot-loosener with me . . ."

What strong knots!

"I'm so glad to see you, spacemice!" I exclaimed. "How did you **FIND** me?"

"It was simple,"

Benjamin replied. "We saw Uncle Trap's gigantic **heavy backpack** and then we followed the trail of sawdust."

Martian mozzarella! I felt so *lucky* that I could count on my friends!

"When we saw the nibblix, we were stunned," Greenfur added. "We didn't know such **aliens** existed on Photosyntheson."

"We used the *Encyclopedia Galactica* to gather a lot of interesting information about the nibblix," squeaked Bugsy Wugsy. "And we found out that they have **a very sweet tooth**."

"That gave me an idea," Thea continued. "I got in touch with the crew on *MouseStar 1* and asked Sally to send us one of Squizzy's **CHEESECAKES** via Teletransportix . . ."

"Not just any cheesecake," Bugsy

specified. "But a **triple cheesecake** with **candied fruit** on top!"

"Exactly!" chuckled Greenfur. "Sally set the Teletransportix so that the cake would be transported right here. Then we lured away the sweet-toothed nibblix with the cake's **mousetastic aroma**!"

Here's the cake!

Stellar Swiss! My friends were truly **out of this world**! Greenfur finally untied the last knot and I was free.

"We'd better get away from here," Thea suggested. "The nibblix will probably be back once they finish eating the cake."

"Wait!" I said. "The nibblix have a real PROBLEM. They need our help!"

The spacemice listened as I explained the situation. Once they heard about the flooded tunnels that had forced the nibblix aliens to abandon their homes, they agreed that we had to help.

"But what can we do for them, Uncle G?" Benjamin asked, a worried look on his snout.

Then we heard a **noise** behind us. The nibblix were back, and they didn't look HAPPY. They were glaring at us and baring their sharp teeth **menacingly**!

WE WANT TO HELP!

Chief Nibbler readjusted his crown, brushed some cake crumbs off his face, and cleared his throat.

"Nibblix, **ELEVATED FORMATION**!" he ordered. "I need to look these gigantic mouseoids in the eye!"

His subjects snapped to work. They quickly began to climb on top of one another's shoulders. It looked like they were building a **strange tower**!

Stinky space cheese! What were they planning to do?

The chief climbed on top of the heap and looked at me, unafraid.

"Geronimo Stiltonix," the chief bellowed. "Who are these mouseoids? **Where** did they come from? And how did you untie yourself?"

"Your Majesty, these are my spacemice friends." I explained.

"Please meet my sister, Thea, my nephew, Benjamin, his friend Bugsy Wugsy, and

Who are they?

They're my friends!

scientist Professor Greenfur."

"We don't want to hurt you," Thea explained. "In fact, my brother told us your story and we want to **help**!"

"We nibblix know how to take care of ourselves!" Chief Nibbler answered proudly.

"But you can't keep gnawing every tree on Photosyntheson!" Professor Greenfur exclaimed. "Before you know it, all the trees will be gone! And many of these trees are home to Photosynthesons who live above ground."

"He's right," Benjamin agreed. "We know the subterranean **tunnels** you live in are in danger, but destroying the habitat of others isn't a good solution. Let us help you. Together we'll find a way to stop the flood in your tunnels!"

The nibblix were silent for a moment.

"What do you propose?" Chief Nibbler finally asked.

"Hmm . . . I think I have an idea," Greenfur mumbled. He began walking **BACK** and *FORTH* in the clearing under the watchful eyes of Chief Nibbler.

I was also **CURIOUS**. What did the professor have in mind?

I've got it!

"**I'VE GOT IT!**" he exclaimed suddenly. "If I could calculate the angle of the tunnels and multiply it by  and divide it by Z, I'll have the solution. But one of you will have to take me to the entrance to the tunnels."

"**And why should we do that?**" Chief Nibbler asked skeptically.

"Because Professor Greenfur is a brilliant

scientist and he's thinking of a way to **save** your homes," I tried to explain. "If you trust him, he might be able to **fix everything**! Then you can go back to living **underground**, where you're **HAPPIEST**!"

The nibblix gathered around their chief. They talked softly for a while. Finally, the **chief** approached me.

"We have decided to *trust you*," he said. "Come! We'll show you the entrance to the **tunnels**."

THE PERFECT PLAN

I put Trap's heavy backpack back on my shoulders, and, for a moment, I wondered what could possibly be inside. But the nibblix scurried ahead quickly and I had to follow, so I didn't get a chance to open the backpack to **FIND OUT**.

Chief Nibbler led us to a part of Photosyntheson we hadn't seen. There was a beautiful garden filled with **star-shaped flowers**. They were so **BEAUTiFUL**! Lots of young nibblix peeked at us through the flowers, staring in **amazement**.

"Fellow nibblix, I present the **Spacemice**!" Chief Nibbler exclaimed. "I granted them the **HONOR** of helping us find a solution to our **flooded** tunnels. Please escort them underground for an INSPECTION!"

As soon as the chief finished talking, a few nibblix came forward to lead the way. We *followed* them to the opening of a large tunnel. Greenfur **examined** the entrance closely.

"The upper TUNNELS are still dry," our guide informed us, "but if we don't stop the water soon, everything will be flooded and we'll have no place to live!"

"What do you have in mind?" I asked the professor.

"I was thinking of building a dam," Professor Greenfur explained. "But first I have to check a few things . . ."

He took out a strange contraption.

"This is a **processorix**," Greenfur

explained. "It's a brilliant invention! You wear it, think about what you want to do, and then the *processorix* formulates a plan for the project at the speed of light. I'll use the device to send a **PROBE** to inspect the interior of the tunnel. The probe will collect the data I need while the processorix picks up the **impulses** from my brain and designs a project automatically on the screen!"

The nibblix were a little **PERPLEXED** by the device (honestly, so was I!), but they went along with Greenfur's plan anyway.

"We got it!" the professor exclaimed happily a few moments later.

Then he showed us an image on the **processorix** screen.

"Every nibblix will bring some sandbags into the tunnel," he explained. "The bags will be used to build a dam near the hole where the water is entering."

We got it!

The nibblix looked at the illustration of the plan on the **processorix**. They seemed very impressed.

"As soon as the DAM reaches the dimensions indicated HERE, the water will stop, and your tunnels will be dry again!" Greenfur concluded.

The nibblix applauded happily.

"But stopping the water won't be enough," Greenfur warned. "The dam could BREAK at some point. The solution is to have a group of nibblix DIG a lateral tunnel next to the original tunnel while the other group is busy hauling in the sandbags."

"But why do we need the second tunnel?" one of the nibblix asked, perplexed.

"If the water **spills out** of

the riverbed, it will run along the secondary tunnel instead of breaking through the dam and **washing away** your homes," Professor Greenfur explained.

"But what happens to the water then?" asked Chief Nibbler.

"At the end of the second tunnel, you'll have to dig a big, deep hole to collect the water," Greenfur said. "That basin can double as an awesome **swimming pool**!"

"Amazing!" exclaimed Chief Nibbler. "Come on, nibblix! We can do this. Now, let's get to work!"

IN THE TUNNELS

The nibblix were about to follow their chief into the tunnels when Benjamin had an idea.

"Uncle!" he cried. "I can give the chief my **Wristwatch** so he can communicate with us while he and the other nibblix are underground."

It was a **FABUMOUSE** idea.

"Hey, Nibbler!" I called out.

The chief turned to me and **incinerated** me with a look.

"Oh, uh, excuse me, Your Majesty," I muttered, my snout turning **red** with embarrassment. "Wait a second, please!"

We **strapped** Benjamin's wristwatch onto Chief Nibbler's small paw, and the aliens went down into the tunnels, each

Here you go!

carrying a **sandbag**. We followed their work from the surface using Thea's wristwatch. I took off the heavy backpack and used it as a seat to rest on.

My sister pushed a button on her wristwatch.

"Your Majesty, can you hear me?" she asked. "How's it going down there?"

"I can hear you loud and clear!" came the king's reply. "We're just getting to the hole where the **water** is coming from. We can't see anything yet, but we know we are close because the ground is damp under our paws."

"Good luck, Chief!" we all shouted.

"**Thank you!**" came the reply of the chief and the other nibblix around him.

"We've rolled the sandbags in position to make the dam. And Crunch and Scrunch, two of the strongest nibblix, have begun to **dig** the lateral tunnel . . ."

"**GREAT!**" we all shouted. "You're almost there. Keep up the **GOOD WORK**!"

"Oh no!" Chief Nibbler said suddenly.

"What's wrong?" asked Thea.

"The water is **leaking through** the dam. We need more sandbags!" Chief Nibbler replied.

"Don't worry!" Benjamin squeaked as he leaped into *action*. "We'll help. Bugsy and I can gather a few more for you."

The two mice SCAMPERED off and returned a few minutes later with a bunch of sandbags. They delivered them to the mouth of the tunnel.

Less than an hour later, Chief Nibbler and

the other nibblix emerged from the tunnel, smiling and **happy**.

"Is everything okay now?" Benjamin asked.

"Never been better!" the chief replied. "The dam and the lateral tunnel are complete. We can return to our homes IMMEDIATELY!"

PHOTOSYNTHESON'S TREES

Benjamin, Bugsy Wugsy, and the nibblix cheered **joyfully**. Thea, Greenfur, and I were ecstatic, too. **Photosyntheson's** homes were safe, and the nibblix could go back to living underground, where they were **HAPPIEST**.

Hooray!

Chief Nibbler shook Professor Greenfur's paw and thanked us.

"It's always a pleasure to help those in **need**!" Greenfur replied.

The chief hung his head.

"I feel badly for the way we treated our fellow Photosynthesons and their **PRECIOUS** trees!" he said sadly.

Thank you, friend!

It was a pleasure!

"We truly didn't mean to **destroy** anyone's homes. But we've always LIVED ALONE underground, and we've never had to think about anyone else. We didn't realize gnawing on all those trees would AFFECT others the way it did. What can we do to make it up to you and your friends, Professor?"

"You could help the Photosynthesons replant the trees you gnawed!" Greenfur suggested.

"That's a great idea!" squeaked Benjamin. "Nature helps improve the universe for everyone. We need to **love**, **respect**, and protect it!"

"You're right!" Chief Nibbler replied. "First we'll ask the Photosynthesons for their FORGIVENESS, and then we will help them plant NEW trees!"

But I noticed that the chief still looked like he had *something* on his mind.

"What is it, Your Majesty?" I asked.

"Well . . ." he hesitated. "We're **very happy** to return to our tunnels and our cozy homes, but I'd like to come back to the surface every so often. It's so **dark** and **gloomy** underground. And now that we've seen how beautiful it is above ground, we would like to visit sometimes. But we can't go for long without *gnawing* on something, so I guess that won't be **possible**."

The other nibblix nodded in agreement, and the chief hung his head *sadly*.

Hmmm . . . what a **TOUGH** situation! There had to be a solution, but what was it?

Greenfur, Thea, Benjamin, Bugsy Wugsy, and I looked at one another. We spacemice needed another MOUSERIFIC idea!

We **thought** and **thought** and **thought** and **thought** and **thought**.

"We have to find something above ground that the nibblix can **chew** without harming anything," Thea mused.

MARTIAN MOZZARELLA! That was easier said than done! What could the nibblix gnaw safely?

I didn't have a clue!

A Gigantic Surprise

After a lot of thinking, we were still stuck.

"Sometimes my best ideas come when I stop concentrating on the *problem* and think of something different!" Benjamin exclaimed.

"That's true!" Thea agreed. "It helps me brainstorm when I move around, take a walk, or *play a game*."

1 I tripped over my own paws . . .

So we all began to walk around. I went in circles, but I was so absorbed in my thoughts that I tripped on my own paws and fell on top of Trap's **HEAVY BACKPACK**! Swisssh!

The backpack flew up in the air and its contents scattered all over the ground.

Galactic mozzarella! What a **mess**!

SWISSSH!

> 2 . . . and fell on top of Trap's backpack!

I was scrambling to collect everything when one object caught my *attention*. It was a gigantic machine that dispensed Supergnaws, also known as chunks of  VEGA CARROTS. They're one of Trap's favorite snacks! My cousin had miniaturized the device before putting it in the backpack, and my fall had triggered the expansion mechanism.

"Trap never changes!" Benjamin chuckled. "Anytime we travel, he always manages to pack something crunchy . . ."

"Did you say 'something crunchy'?" asked Greenfur. "Why didn't we think of that before?"

Huh? Thought of what? I didn't have a clue what the professor was squeaking about.

But Thea understood.

"Of course!" she exclaimed. "You're a genius, Professor Greenfur!"

The scientist turned to Chief Nibbler. "**Your Majesty**, we have the solution!" he announced happily. "We are proud to present you and the nibblix with this **Supergnaw distributor**! Supergnaws are yummy pieces of Vega carrots. Munching on them will be **great** for keeping your teeth *busy* while you're above ground!"

I finally understood.

"That's right!" I exclaimed.

"And Vega carrots aren't just great for the teeth, they're also rich in

Here's the solution!

galactic vitamins. Eating them will keep your whole body **HEALTHY**!"

"And best of all, this machine will dispense an **endless supply**!" Benjamin chimed in, smiling **BRIGHTLY**.

"So we won't have to gnaw on trees anymore?" Chief Nibbler asked, astounded. "Crunchy underground dirt! What a **great idea**!"

The other nibblix agreed.

"Thank you, spacemice!" they shouted happily. "What a **generous** gift!

"Now we'll be able to come above ground whenever we like!" Chief Nibbler exclaimed.

To Plant a Tree . . .

Now that the nibblix were no longer a **threat** to Photosyntheson's trees, we were anxious to tell all the Photosynthesons the good news. We used our wristwatches to contact Leafyfur, and we arranged a meeting in Evergreen Grove. When we got to the park, we found Leafyfur and a huge **CROWD** of Photosynthesons waiting for us.

Greenfur told everyone what had happened. Then he introduced **Chief Nibbler** and the nibblix to the Photosynthesons.

The chief apologized many times for what the nibblix had done to the planet's **precious** trees. He sounded nothing like the alien who had taken me **PRISONER** earlier!

"We didn't realize how **important** the trees are to you," Chief Nibbler explained. "But we are grateful to the spacemice for teaching us. And we now understand that we have to respect and love nature."

"We accept your APOLOGIES, friends!" said Leafyfur.

Everyone was happy. Leafyfur and Chief Nibbler SHOOK paws as a sign of friendship and collaboration.

"We'd like to make things up to you by replanting the trees we *DESTROYED*," the chief of the nibblix explained.

The Photosynthesons accepted happily.

"From now on, Photosynthesons and nibblix will live in

From now on, we'll be friends!

Thank you!

harmony, **respecting nature!**"

Everyone cheered. Then Leafyfur turned on a giant **seed-spreader** and gave handfuls of seeds to all of us.

We headed for the section of the park where the nibblix had **GNAWED** the trees. Together we began to spread the seeds.

Seeds for everyone!

Eventually, we came to the place where Greenfur's OLD TREE once stood.

"You spread here," I told my friend. "Soon a new tree will grow, and it will be *stronger* than the one before it!"

Professor Greenfur THREW a handful of seeds on the ground. Lush little plants began to sprout INSTANTLY. At the same time, the scientist's fur turned from orange to green again, from the top of his head to the tips of his toes!

Out-of-orbit planets! Our mission was complete!

THE KEY TO HAPPINESS

In addition to spreading seeds, the nibblix also helped plant some tiny trees. When the work was complete, Leafyfur organized a **big celebration** in Evergreen Grove. It was a superstellar event because the Photosynthesons and the nibblix **worked**

Hooray!

Yummy!

together to plan the entire thing.

There were huge **TABLES** with Photosyntheson specialties and crunchy foods that were perfect for the nibblix. We played **games** and gathered in a clearing to celebrate the friendship between the Photosynthesons and the nibblix with a **toe-tapping dance**!

Starry skies! It was a truly **spectacular** event!

Do you want to dance?

Here are some carrots!

As the festivities came to an end, we spacemice got ready to **Leave**.

Violix and **Gentiana** hugged Greenfur.

"Come back soon!" they squeaked.

"**I WILL — I PROMISE!**" the professor replied, tears in his eyes. "I understand now that my bond with my home planet is a **strong** one that can never be **broken**!"

"Well said!" Chief Nibbler bellowed. "We would love to see you again soon, especially since our subterranean dam will need to be **inspected** from time to time to be sure it's holding up okay!"

"Yes, the spacemice are always welcome here!" Leafyfur agreed. "We shall always be **GRATEFUL** to you for saving our planet!"

"No, no," I replied. "We should be thanking all of you! This mission taught us that living in HARMONY with nature is truly the key to happiness!"

Then we said good-bye and boarded the space shuttle that would take us back to *MouseStar 1*, and toward another **INCREDIBLE NEW ADVENTURE**!

Good-bye, friends!

Don't miss any adventures of the Spacemice!

#1 Alien Escape

#2 You're Mine, Captain!

#3 Ice Planet Adventure

#4 The Galactic Goal

#5 Rescue Rebellion

#6 The Underwater Planet

#7 Beware! Space Junk!

#8 Away in a Star Sled

#9 Slurp Monster Showdown

#10 Pirate Spacecat Attack

#11 We'll Bite Your Tail, Geronimo!

#12 The Invisible Planet

MEET
Geronimo Stiltonord

He is a mouseking — the Geronimo Stilton of the ancient far north! He lives with his brawny and brave clan in the village of Mouseborg. From sailing frozen waters to facing fiery dragons, every day is an adventure for the micekings!

#1 Attack of the Dragons

#2 The Famouse Fjord Race

#3 Pull the Dragon's Tooth!

#4 Stay Strong, Geronimo!

#5 The Mysterious Message

#6 The Helmet Holdup

Be sure to read all my fabumouse adventures!

#1 Lost Treasure of the Emerald Eye

#2 The Curse of the Cheese Pyramid

#3 Cat and Mouse in a Haunted House

#4 I'm Too Fond of My Fur!

#5 Four Mice Deep in the Jungle

#6 Paws Off, Cheddarface!

#7 Red Pizzas for a Blue Count

#8 Attack of the Bandit Cats

#9 A Fabumouse Vacation for Geronimo

#10 All Because of a Cup of Coffee

#11 It's Halloween, You 'Fraidy Mouse!

#12 Merry Christmas, Geronimo!

#13 The Phantom of the Subway

#14 The Temple of the Ruby of Fire

#15 The Mona Mousa Code

#16 A Cheese-Colored Camper

#17 Watch Your Whiskers, Stilton!

#18 Shipwreck on the Pirate Islands

#19 My Name Is Stilton, Geronimo Stilton

#20 Surf's Up, Geronimo!

#21 The Wild, Wild West

#22 The Secret of Cacklefur Castle

A Christmas Tale

#23 Valentine's Day Disaster

#24 Field Trip to Niagara Falls

#25 The Search for Sunken Treasure

#26 The Mummy with No Name

#27 The Christmas Toy Factory

#28 Wedding Crasher

#29 Down and Out Down Under

#30 The Mouse Island Marathon

#31 The Mysterious Cheese Thief

Christmas Catastrophe

#32 Valley of the Giant Skeletons

#33 Geronimo and the Gold Medal Mystery

#34 Geronimo Stilton, Secret Agent

#35 A Very Merry Christmas

#36 Geronimo's Valentine

#37 The Race Across America

#38 A Fabumouse School Adventure

#39 Singing Sensation

#40 The Karate Mouse

#41 Mighty Mount Kilimanjaro

#42 The Peculiar Pumpkin Thief

#43 I'm Not a Supermouse!

#44 The Giant Diamond Robbery

#45 Save the White Whale!

#46 The Haunted Castle

#47 Run for the Hills, Geronimo!

#48 The Mystery in Venice

#49 The Way of the Samurai

#50 This Hotel Is Haunted!

#51 The Enormouse Pearl Heist

#52 Mouse in Space!

#53 Rumble in the Jungle

#54 Get into Gear, Stilton!

#55 The Golden Statue Plot

#56 Flight of the Red Bandit

The Hunt for the Golden Book

#57 The Stinky Cheese Vacation

#58 The Super Chef Contest

#59 Welcome to Moldy Manor

The Hunt for the Curious Cheese

#60 The Treasure of Easter Island

#61 Mouse House Hunter

#62 Mouse Overboard!

The Hunt for the Secret Papyrus

#63 The Cheese Experiment

#64 Magical Mission

#65 Bollywood Burglary

The Hunt for the Hundredth Key

#66 Operation: Secret Recipe

#67 The Chocolate Chase

Don't miss any of my adventures in the Kingdom of Fantasy!

THE KINGDOM OF FANTASY

THE QUEST FOR PARADISE:
THE RETURN TO THE KINGDOM OF FANTASY

THE AMAZING VOYAGE:
THE THIRD ADVENTURE IN THE KINGDOM OF FANTASY

THE DRAGON PROPHECY:
THE FOURTH ADVENTURE IN THE KINGDOM OF FANTASY

THE VOLCANO OF FIRE:
THE FIFTH ADVENTURE IN THE KINGDOM OF FANTASY

THE SEARCH FOR TREASURE:
THE SIXTH ADVENTURE IN THE KINGDOM OF FANTASY

THE ENCHANTED CHARMS:
THE SEVENTH ADVENTURE IN THE KINGDOM OF FANTASY

THE PHOENIX OF DESTINY:
AN EPIC KINGDOM OF FANTASY ADVENTURE

THE HOUR OF MAGIC:
THE EIGHTH ADVENTURE IN THE KINGDOM OF FANTASY

THE WIZARD'S WAND:
THE NINTH ADVENTURE IN THE KINGDOM OF FANTASY

THE SHIP OF SECRETS:
THE TENTH ADVENTURE IN THE KINGDOM OF FANTASY

THE DRAGON OF FORTUNE:
AN EPIC KINGDOM OF FANTASY ADVENTURE

Don't miss any of these exciting Thea Sisters adventures!

Thea Stilton and the Dragon's Code

Thea Stilton and the Mountain of Fire

Thea Stilton and the Ghost of the Shipwreck

Thea Stilton and the Secret City

Thea Stilton and the Mystery in Paris

Thea Stilton and the Cherry Blossom Adventure

Thea Stilton and the Star Castaways

Thea Stilton: Big Trouble in the Big Apple

Thea Stilton and the Ice Treasure

Thea Stilton and the Secret of the Old Castle

Thea Stilton and the Blue Scarab Hunt

Thea Stilton and the Prince's Emerald

Thea Stilton and the Mystery on the Orient Express

Thea Stilton and the Dancing Shadows

Thea Stilton and the Legend of the Fire Flowers

Thea Stilton and the Spanish Dance Mission

Thea Stilton and the Journey to the Lion's Den

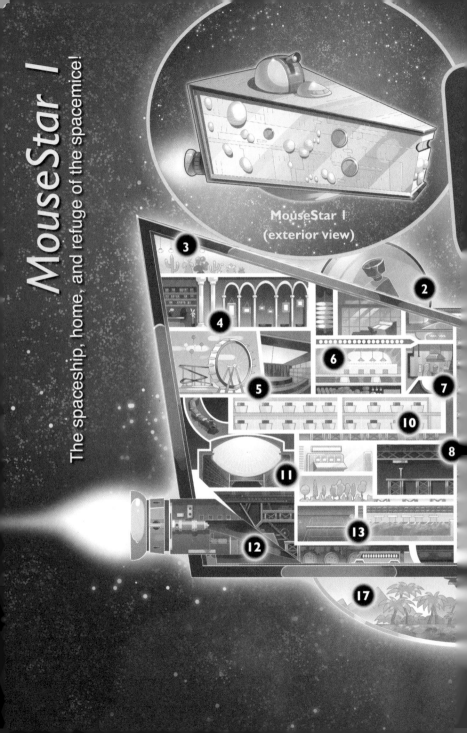

1. Control room
2. Gigantic telescope
3. Greenhouse to grow plants and flowers
4. Library and reading room
5. Astral Park, an amusement park
6. Space Yum Café
7. Kitchen
8. Liftrix, the special elevator that moves between all floors of the spaceship
9. Computer room
10. Crew cabins
11. Theater for space shows
12. Warp-speed engines
13. Tennis court and swimming pool
14. Multipurpose technogym
15. Space pods for exploration
16. Cargo hold for food supply
17. Natural biosphere

Dear mouse friends,
thanks for reading,
and good-bye until the next book.
See you in outer space!